BEASTCALL: A PALADINS OF THE HARVEST NOVELLA

KADEN LOVE

CONTENTS

For my parents
To mom, who comforted and guided me to overcome
every obstacle and worry
To dad, the best coach and teacher who taught me how
to live

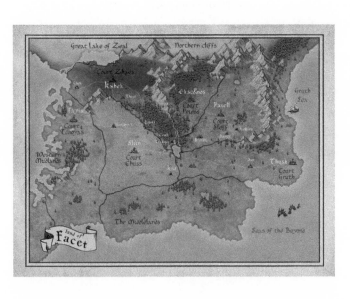

GLOSSARY

Beastling: Endowers that can speak with animals.

Bronze Seers: Organization known to work outside of the law.

Buyak: Creature that is vulpine in appearance with no fur and small tentacles coming from its mane.

Canton: A building and institution led by a Thane under their respective responsibility.

Cloven Gleff: Center of Facet's mining. Site of export for Zhaes bronze, among other metals. Located near Kzhek.

Court: One of the six fiefdoms that make up the continent of Facet.

- Sleff

    - Banner: Yellow banner with a black spinerat

    - Salute: Place the heels of the palms on the temples and extend the fingers upward

    - Ideal: *Pious is the Giver*

- Values: Humility, meekness

- Scripture: The Tome of the Meek

- God: Heitt

• Tchoyas

- Banner Blue putle on a light gray banner

- Salute: Interwoven fingers covering the mouth

- Ideal: *Steadfast is the Honor*

- Values: Loyalty, honor

- Scripture: The Tome of Piety

- God: Klen

• Zhaes

- Banner: Bronze Kaesan on a dark gray banner

- Salute: Steepled fingers over the face, pointing upwards

- Ideal: *Whole is the Holy*

- Values: Obedience, perfection

- Scripture: The Tome of Measure

- God: Laeih

- Gruth

  - Banner: Green leviathan eel on a teal banner

  - Salute: Elbows against the torso, bent at ninety degrees, fists clenched, as if bracing for a strike to the abdomen

  - Ideal: *Firm is the foundation*

  - Values: Endurance, strength

  - Scripture: The Tome of Stability

  - God: Deilf

- Chuss

  - Banner: Crimson ghete on a white banner

  - Salute: Hands creating a circle and placed over the center of the chest

  - Ideal: *Care is the creed*

- Values: Love, charity

- Scripture: The Tome of Charity

- God: Cheric

- Priess

  - Banner: Gold land eel on a purple banner

  - Salute: Right ear cupped as if trying to hear, left arm raised in a fist

  - Ideal: Mighty is the free

  - Values: Pride, liberation

  - Export: textiles

  - No scripture or god

Endower: Children born with an additional intestine, granting them a "god-sent" ability. The cardinal sign is a second umbilical cord at birth. Reports state that many do not survive past their first year of life. Four of the six Courts harvest these organs to be grafted into an adult Endowed.

Endowed: An individual who has received a graft from an Endower in order to gain their congenital ability.

Eurythrin: Endowers who can halt blood flow, regenerate, and help heal.

Facet: Continent composed of six Courts. Its boundaries do not include the Middlelands or nations beyond the northern cliffs.

Feelman: An Endower who can read people's emotions by identifying their bodily functions, correctly predict their next move, and almost read their mind.

Ghete: Reptilian steeds that share are described as "a large cat with green scales and no ears."

Gorger: Endower with increased growth, including of the mind and muscle.

Harvest: The medical process of removing an Endowed intestine from an Endower at birth. This intestine will then be grafted into an adult, making them an Endowed.

Krall: Monarch of a Court.

Patriarchy of Scholars: A Scholarly society that is not deterred by Court boundaries. They are said to promote unity and societal growth, though they are very exclusive and do not reveal their works to those outside of their ranks.

Thane: An elect individual that serves over a specific office of a Court. The only office higher than a Thane is that of a Court's Krall. Members of the nobility.

- Offices include the Thanes of:

- Utilities: Technological advancements, engineering

- Veneration: Religious practices and law

- Haleness: Medicinal practice and health promotion

- Diplomacy: Diplomatic matters with foreign Courts

- Scholarship: Represent the Patriarchy of Scholars and all scholarly pursuits

- Agriculture: Livestock, metals, crops, and all other natural materials

- Progress: Politics, anthropology, and innovation

- Endowment: Harvesting and Endowed in Courts that permit the process. Courts who oppose harvesting manage Endower growth, usage, and study.

Dramatis Personae

Horrah: Healer in service to the Zhaes nobility

Kael: Runith's assistant

Rhen: Gorger in service to the Zhaes nobility

Royss Belik: Zhaes Thane of Agriculture

Runith: Captain of Thane Royss Belik's guard

Sheath Leisa: Zhaes Thane of Diplomacy

Tholn: Zhaes Proctor of ore, leads labor at the Cloven Gleff

Yeila: Gorger in service to the Zhaes nobility

I *am not proud of my past. I've killed nuisances to cities and villages, that much I accept, but I've also killed some beautiful beasts. I've slain those worthy of a tranquil dream. The kind our gods created as living artwork.*

Runith looked up from his reverie. An eldeer buck as large as a tavern crossed a damp field. Its antlers brushed leaves, caressing them.

I'm grateful for change, yet I still loathe the barbarian I once was.

Now, I tame beasts having sworn off senseless slaughter. I'm a Beastling, one given the gift of speaking with all living beings. I am part of nature, no longer its bane.

Despite the pain, I find value in reflecting upon who I was before my graft before I learned the beastcall.

CHAPTER ONE

BLOODY GILLS

FOUR YEARS AGO – YEAR 328 IN THE CLERICAL ERA

"I live to slay! By Laeih, I was born to kill!" Runith shouted as he pummeled his great sword through the skull of the fleeing zein, the other rogue zeins began to retreat. Their webbed feet sped across the marsh much quicker than Runith in his ankle-high hunting boots. He'd never taken a liking to their species. A humanoid fish was something from a dream after too many drinks.

"You've stolen... hurt—" He wiped their dark blood from his hands across his short beard, turning to his young shield bearer. "What did they do again?."

"Ate the elderly, sir. You should know that," replied Kael, scratching his dark, curly hair.

Runith arched his thick eyebrows. "Really?"

Kael nodded.

"You know, I'm paid to not ask questions, but I feel like I have a duty to punish these wet kulfs." He turned his head back toward them, Kael falling behind their sprint after the two remaining zeins. "You've eaten enough people. It's time to pay!" *Perd, I sound like a sappy hero in a bard's tale.*

The fish-men fled across the mud, some tripping as they turned to hear Runith's call, though they did not understand human-speak.

Their school of zeins split as they approached a large, green pond. Their squeals grew louder as Runith closed the distance between his blade and the rightmost group.

He raised his sword against the slowest among them, but missed his strike as they dove into the pond, becoming lost in the moss and black lilies.

He turned to run around the pond to catch the other half of the group. He was too slow as they joined the others below the water.

Kael panted, his map twisting in the wind as he ran to stand beside Runith. Kael fell to a crouch, wiping the fog off of his spectacles as Runith stared at the water.

"At..." Kael spat phlegm after a coughing fit, the trail lingering from his mouth and falling to his shoes. "At least we got some of them."

"Doesn't matter," Runith said. "They'll go right back to eating. As long as they cause problems, we won't be paid a single coin."

"I know, I know, but maybe you could—"

With the roar of a waterfall, a giant humanoid of scales and fins stood from the pond. The splash covered Runith and Kael in the pond's black and green grime.

Kael ran to hide among the trees, leaving his map in the mud. Runith unsheathed two short swords from his scabbards, laughing like a madman.

The creature stood in the pond with water up to its knees. Despite its form with two arms, two legs, a head, and a tail, it was no single being. It was a conglomeration of interlocked zeins, rising higher than a chapel. Some tails led to mouths, some arms twined with legs as if they had no bones to restrict their movement. The distorted faces of the zeins were smashed, yet each eye watched Runith.

"Runith, I really think we shou—"

"Kael! Grab the salt!"

Heavy legs made of at least ten zeins trod from the center of the pond.

Kael tore through the bag with shaking hands. "How much? I don't know if—"

"All of it!"

He tossed Runith two jars filled with a viscous pink fluid.

Runith caught the first, dropping the second at his left foot, while he held his swords with his armpit. The second jar fell halfway into a mud pocket.

He struck the first jar with one of the swords and raised it, letting the pink liquid ooze down the blade. He then shattered the second jar in the mud and dipped his other blade into the jar's remains, coating it in a blend of pink liquid and brown mud.

"Die, you wet *kulf*!" Runith roared as he approached the pond.

"Do we have to use profanity, sir?" Kael peeked behind draping vines.

"If anything deserves to be called a kulf, it's this mess of flesh."

The beast hissed from each mouth in its mountain of fins and gills.

It stepped from the water, sinking to its ankles in mud, while Runith only dirtied the brim of his boots.

He roared as he ran at the beast with his hair flowing back.

The chain of creatures that functioned as hands swung at him with the speed of a darting lobster.

Runith lifted his sword, striking the arms with his pink-coated blade. Everything depended on the pink salt substance to break the wetland beast apart.

Though he cut deep, he was thrown onto the far bank of the water as if the creature tossed a pebble.

"Runith?" Kael called as his superior lay still in the mud. "Runith!"

The zein conglomeration turned away from Runith and towards his alcove of vines. "*Mother of a bloody wet kulf!*" Kael screamed.

Runith pushed himself up from the mud. "Prreerol-lll."

"I can't hear you!" Kael ran through trees around the pond's circumference, hoping his pursuer would stumble.

Trees fell like trampled twigs in its wake. The creature dominated its surroundings as a king in its murky realm.

"Pull out a *perding* bolt!" Mud flew from Runith's beard as he shouted.

Kael flung his arms behind his back, reaching for his crossbow, and loaded a bolt with the tip the size of a spear from his hip-side quiver. Shaking hands aimed as the beast drew closer to Kael. Puddles splashed like tidal waves.

"Shoot it, you kulf!" Runith shouted.

Kael pulled the trigger and launched the head-heavy bolt in an arc into the center of the beast's chest.

The bolt's tip shattered as it buried itself in the center of the beast's breast. The pink salt-toxin encasing the tip would stream through the zeins' interconnected veins. A crash and sizzle emanated from the wound, like a pot of water shattering onto orange-glowing steel.

The behemoth contorted and wailed as the wound left a black mark on its flesh. The giant separated, falling back into individual zeins that screeched and clawed at their bodies, convulsing.

Runith stood and limped with a hanging left arm, using his remaining strength to end their gurgling screams with the blade in his right hand. Slow and thorough, he paved a path of carnage.

Runith sliced the neck of the last one, falling to his knees in the mud.

⟫⟫⟫⟫ ⟨⟨⟨⟨

"Again, Runith?" Royss Belik, the Thane of Agriculture for Court Zhaes paced behind his desk. "How many times is Kael going to have to drag you back here? I can't have the captain of my guard gambling his life on beast hunts."

"We brought the salt jars. I even put salt on my blades! You know how those freshwater bastards shrivel up with salt." Runith rebutted as he acted out the slashes of his swords from a seat across Royss' desk. Runith remained seated, still fatigued from the previous day's hunt.

"That doesn't matter. I cannot have you taking contracts to hunt down the menaces of insignificant villages. We live in *Kzhek,* the capital of Court Zhaes. Those problems are for the farmers and the villagers' protection."

"You're the perding Thane of Agriculture, leading the Court's agricultural stability. Shouldn't that be important to you?"

"That is beside the point."

Runith smirked, knowing that he had frustrated his friend. Even though Royss—or *Thane Belik,* as he was called—was higher in Zhaes nobility, they were still friends. Unfortunately, the chair across from Royss' desk had grown quite accustomed to Runith as of late.

"Don't we pay you enough to not worry about risking your life as a beast hunter?" Royss scowled, pausing his pacing.

"Yes, payment is no concern."

"Then what is it?"

"I enjoy slaying the ugly beasts. The thrill of it is better than any mead or drink I've ever had."

"By Laeih's holy name." Royss returned to shaking his head, resigned to sitting at his desk. "This is the fifth time that you've nearly died, and at least the fourth broken bone."

"It'll be the sixth scar from hunts, too." *Sixth scar not covered by clothing.*

Royss' chuckle escaped, but only for a moment. "I need you here, protecting the Canton. Harvesting has begun throughout the six Courts, you know that, right?"

"That thing with the younglings? Taking their guts out for magic?"

"Runith, this is going to change Facet and its Courts more than any event in history. This is not simply a 'thing' with 'magic'. Do you understand what harvesting is?"

He shrugged. Royss assaulted him with a pensive glare. Runith shook his head.

"The Cantons of Haleness throughout Facet have found a way to remove the endowed intestine. Yes, the one that grants a supernatural ability. We can remove this from a newborn and implant it in an adult, therefore granting them the ability."

"But won't that kill the infant?"

"Yes... but sacrifices must be made. Most of the elect-born die before their first name day, or so I have been told. To ignore this opportunity would be a disgrace."

"Why does this concern me?"

"Two of the six Courts oppose this process. Courts Chuss and Tchoyas refuse the proposed law of *requiring* this organ harvest. I am concerned about their vehement opposition and problems it could create."

"So, war?"

"No, no, we are not savages. Still, that does not discount the occasional violent activist. Political contentions are growing. I would appreciate the maturity of the *captain* of my guard to focus on protecting his Thane and the Krall we serve."

Runith sighed and nodded.

"What is it with you?" Royss squinted and jabbed him with an accusatory finger. "You're a perding Zhaesman. We should strive for righteousness rather than brutality."

"Well, I've never killed another human."

"I would argue that some of those creatures are smarter than you."

Runith feigned a chuckle. Why not slay a man if he deserves it? Would he enjoy it just as much as slaying a beast? What glory would war bring him? "Fair point. I suppose those magi are the only ones who could tell us."

"Magi?"

"You were just talking about them, Royss! Those people who take an organ graft for."

"The Endowed?"

"So that's what we are calling them?"

"Yes, and they are not magi. I still don't know what you were talking about."

Runith fanned out his hands to defend himself. "And you say I am the ignorant one! I've heard about those 'Endowed.' Some of them are big and strong, some can read minds, some can talk to animals. Surely they could tell us how I'm smarter than the zeins or imps that I've slain."

"They can't exactly *read* minds, but I suppose you are not too far off. Those are the common strains, but I have heard of other types."

Runith placed his hands on the chair's arms and leaned forward. "Anything else? I should probably head home for some rest."

"Just stay away from the beasts. Please."

"You know, I wouldn't have to kill them if I could talk to them. Maybe in a few years I could become one of the Endowed." Runith chuckled as he stood to leave.

"Maybe," Royss muttered.

CHAPTER TWO

A TASTE OF GLORY

"Heloath."

"Heloath."

"Heloath."

Runith greeted those who entered the Canton of Agriculture with the enthusiasm of a mortician.

"You know you're a guard, not a greeter, right?"

Runith turned to Teas–the guard on the other side of the door–with a dry stare.

"I know, but I need something to do. Have you ever had to apprehend anyone? Defend anyone?"

"No, but—"

"If I was a thief, I would seek the Canton of Utilities. What could they steal from us, seeds?"

"Bronze." Teas said. "Royss has jurisdiction over the Cloven Gleff."

"And what would you do with ore? I never thought you would be a smith."

"I..."

Runith Smirked. "Find me something else to do and I will gladly comply." He turned back to face the street. "Perd you, Teas. Two Zhaesmen have entered without a proper greeting. I'll have to make up for that later."

Teas rolled his eyes, and Runith returned to his routine.

"Heloath."

"Heloath."

"Helo—"

"Runith?" a voice called from inside the Canton.

"Yes?"

"Royss would like to see you."

Runith left without question. As the door closed, he heard Taes greet all those who entered the Canton.

⋘⋙

"You wanted me?" Runith said as he entered Royss' study. "Finally surrendering to the hunt?"

"Yes." Royss replied.

Runith laughed, then furrowed his brow as Royss remained serious. "Are you perding serious?"

"Yes, but it might not be how you expected."

Runith swung a chair back and fell onto its cushion. "Well, what do you want me to slay? I'll take anything, just don't send me to Chuss. My knuckles tend to bleed around this time of year and the desert only makes it worse."

"You'll stay here, don't worry, but I don't want you to kill this time."

"I know you're the Thane of Agriculture, but I don't want to give up guard duty for cattle care."

"Runith, are you going to listen or just fill my ears with your poor humor? Perd, you sound like a child sometimes."

Runith drew his lips tight and nodded.

"I want you to continue 'protecting,' as you say. Rather than killing these beasts, I think we can make use of them. I want you to be the first Beastling in service of the Canton of Agriculture."

"*Beastling*, what in Laeih's name is that?"

"A branch of the Endowed"

"You want to cut me open and give me a new organ to—"

"Beastlings can communicate with humans, animals, and other beasts. Language is no barrier. And yes, that would require that you have a new organ grafted into you."

"I don't know about that, Royss. I'm not too keen about... sharp objects." Runith pressed the sword at his side behind him, noticing Royss' confused scowl."

"Don't worry, an Eurythrin will put you to sleep and halt the blood flow before opening you for placement."

"Ah yes, the Eur..."

"Eurythrin. By Laeih's sake Runith, do you follow anything that is going in the Courts? Our land will never be the same. Grafting, though still new, has been enforced for a year and has already proved to catalyze societal growth."

"What do you expect? I stand guard and hunt."

Royss replied with a stare.

"I know, I know. I should pay attention. I'll see to that, noting that you want me to become one. Might you remind me which ones are the Eurythrins?"

"They halt blood flow, can manipulate certain bodily functions, and are capable of surviving nearly any wound."

"So they would make this process safe?"

"Safer than giving birth."

"That's not saying much, Royss."

"It is safer now, except for the Endowers that tend to die."

"Endowers? Have you created your own language? No... wait, I remember that one. Those are the children born with these *special* organs, right?"

"Right. We harvest their organs because many of them tend to die before their first name day. This allows us to give their abilities to adults that can utilize these powers. Think of how great a mercy that is. These children can live on in the body of someone who can wield their powers. This is a *gift* to the recipient and the grieving parents alike. The Eurythrins can learn the organ's function upon the harvest. That is how we know which power we grant to their host or the *Endowed*, as they are now being called. I can forgive you for not being familiar with that term. I've only heard it commonly used recently. Sounds a bit nicer than 'host' in my opinion."

Runtih stroked his beard, nodding. "I think I am beginning to grasp it, but don't throw me out if I ask more questions."

"No promises," Royss smirked.

Runith let loose a tenacious grip from the armrests of his seat. Royss was a close friend, more amiable than most, but he could bite like a viper if pushed beyond his limits.

"So, the child would die anyway, right? The one that they are using?"

"Most likely." Royss avoided eye contact. "Some are bound to survive, that is why the Chussmen and Tchoyasmen outlaw harvesting in their Courts. While some may live, many would die without utilizing this gift. A waste. It is better to harvest than to risk losing a divine gift from Laeih."

"I suppose so." Children began to manifest these abilities only a few years ago, and it had only been a year since this 'harvesting' was initiated. How much could truly be known about how many lived and died?

"So, you will take the organ?" Royss returned his gaze to face Runith.

"Those beasts need hunting, or control. Who else is more fit for the job?"

"I could name a few–"

"Yes, I'll do it. How soon are they expecting to cut me open?"

"Once the Chuss surgeons arrive."

"Why Chussmen?"

"They have done the most research with the Eurythrins. Chuss has always been the capital of medicine."

"Right. '*Care is the Creed*,' as their Ideal states. I thought you said they oppose harvesting?"

"They do. I had the same concern, but the Thane of Veneration told me that they participate to maintain peace with our Court during this era of contention."

Runith opened his eyes and stared at the floor as if he had just been awakened by a thunderstorm.

"Are you well?" Royss asked.

"Yes, it is just a lot to take in." He shook his head. "I failed to recognize how ignorant I was."

"No need to worry. I suppose most of the population is just as ignorant. Soon enough, this will be as normal as Zhaes rain."

"Are you in line to receive one of these organs, Royss?"

"It has been a point of discussion, but you are my present concern."

"So, this Chussman surgeon. When is he or she going to arrive?"

"Tomorrow."

CHAPTER THREE

BUYAK

R unith palpated the purple scar on his abdomen.

"Put your shirt down, we are in public!" Kael whisper-shouted.

Runith continued to press it. "Just a tavern. It's not like we're in the Krall's palace."

"Do you feel it?"

"Oddly enough, not at all. Still feels like the same gut I've had for my whole life."

"How long has it been? Five days?"

"Three." Runith lowered his shirt, smirking as Kael rested back in his seat. The boy was too easy to agitate. He took a pull on his mead as Kael sipped from a steaming teacup.

"That does not make sense."

"How so?"

"Wounds like that take months to heal."

Runith shrugged. "Must be the *Eurythins*. They put me to sleep and stopped the bleeding. It only makes sense that they made it heal quickly. Or maybe it is just a part of my new ability."

"Have you used it yet?"

"Yeah, I told your swine of a mother to bed me." Kael shrank into his chair with red cheeks. Runith could tell the difference between Kael's blushing discomfort and taking offense. He had struck the latter. "I jest, I jest. I've never met your mother and I assume she is a wonderful woman and very beautiful at that." Kael's face grew from a warm sunset to blood red. Too far in the other direction. "I take back all that I said. Enough. None of this happened. No, I have not done anything with the new organ, as far as I have noticed. I'm waiting for Royss to direct me. He allotted me a few days to recover, but it seems like I won't need them. I'm heading to the Canton this evening if you want to join."

"You know, I would like to come."

"Maybe we can talk him into getting you one of these 'gifts.'"

He expected Kael to return to agitation, but the boy smirked at the suggestion. "So, is Thane Beli–"

"Kael, if you want to be comfortable with the man, just call him Royss."

"But he is the Thane of Agriculture! Surely he–"

"He is not as insistent on titles as the other Thanes. Sheath or *Thane Leisa*, does not seem to care for the title either, at least to those who know her. Sorry for the interruption. I've been trying to work on that. We all have our own sins, do we not?"

"Right you are, I too–"

"So, what were you going to say?" Runith took a pull on his mead, looking up from his glass as the drink sifted through his dense mustache.

"Is, um... Royss... planning on recruiting or *making* any more of these *Beastlings* to work with you?"

"It didn't sound like he planned on it, but I suppose we'll see. Seems like these *Endowed* are spread across Zhaes and the Courts that endorse harvesting, but Royss is finally getting his first taste of having one in his service."

"I suppose it's hard to justify giving that kind of power to the Canton that oversees food and land."

"You know we do more than that in the Canton of Agriculture." Runith drew a scowl, though it was more from an itch than in anger.

"You are the one that works for them, Runith. You pay me, or I suppose, give me a share of the bounty from our hunts. I'm not a part of the Canton of Agriculture like you." Kael took a sip from his tea as the steam diminished.

"Perd, I'm not much of a part of it either. I just provide guard work."

"Maybe with this ability, you will be a more significant part of it. Climb the ranks."

"I like the way you think. Maybe we could work you into joining the work there."

They shared a nod, taking a moment to look into their drinks.

"Kael, why do you bother with hunting? No offense, but you seem too..."

"I know. I have more of a bookish personality."

"So why do you do it?"

"Like you said, we all have our sins, our weaknesses. You might think that I'm timid and passive, but I've come a long way. I have a lot to work on if I am ever to be like you."

Runith chucked, bubbles rose in his mead as it drained into his mouth.

❦

Runith had taken Kael into the Canton of Agriculture on other occasions, but never into the upper chambers. Runith barely had the authority to walk there himself.

Kael's eyes drank in the fine decor through his round spectacles. Statues of former Thanes lined the tall halls, each cast in Zhaes bronze. Paintings of Zhaes landscapes were spaced across the walls, depicting high mountains and overcast plains.

As captain of the Canton's guard, he visited these hallways often to meet with Royss. He overlooked the beauty but felt a shimmer of tranquility as he observed Kael's appreciation for otherwise routine sights.

They passed by council rooms and Proctors' offices, finally reaching Royss' chamber for the high council of Agriculture. To their surprise, not a single chair was occupied.

Runith entered, spotting a small note on the table scribbled with Royss' poor penmanship. *Meet in the Courtyard. Waiting for you, Beastling.* He gave the note to Kael who inspected it and left with Runith to descend the stairwell and exit through the back doors of the Canton.

Royss stood in the center of the jousting courtyard beside a burly woman twice his size, a smaller woman in decorative gray robes, and a man who looked to be a farmhand by day and of a less-than-legal occupation by night.

"Glad you could find us!" Royss shouted and his companions turned to face Runith and Kael.

"It would have been easier if you just invited us here rather than to the upper chambers."

"It would have been ideal, but I did not expect Thraen to arrive so early." He motioned to the man at his side, who offered a slight bow with a condescending sneer.

Runith kept his eyes on him, taking the man's visage in as they neared. He was surprised to see someone like him with the Thane of Agriculture. He wore a thin bronze circlet that lined his forehead with a shining eye in the center. The kind worn by a high-ranking member of the Bronze Seers. Their society seemed a poor replication of the Patriarchy of Scholars. Both prided themselves on their exclusivity, though the Patriarchy prided themselves on unified scholarship, while Seers tended to delve into workings beyond the law and outside of governmental jurisdiction.

"Whole is the Holy," spoke Thraen. Each word was elevated, as if he was protruding his jaw out to pontificate, making the Zhaes ideal sound like a crude lie. This was no lowly criminal, but one who placed thieves and whoremongers like pieces on a gameboard. Any Zhaesman would report the labor of a Bronze Seer underling, but their high council members could move past the wall of the law uninhibited.

Runith offered him the Zhaes salute with steepled fingers pointed up and placed over his face. He returned it with a dry gesture. Runith could get along well with anyone, regardless of their profession, but this man seeped sanctimony and vile intentions.

It was easy to divert his attention to the other two beside Royss. "And who might these two beautiful Zhaeswomen be?"

The large woman smirked, while the robed woman offered a timid smile beneath her hood, curled black hair falling out each side like a celestial waterfall. Her gaze was comforting, warm like a faint ray of sunshine in a sky of moving clouds.

"Yeila is the Gorger, and—"

"So," Runith interrupted with an arched eyebrow at Yeila, "you're one of us?"

"You look small for a Gorger, you must be new." She replied with a sneer. Her piercing green eyes took a bite from Runith's ego. He was tall by Zhaes standards, yet she still stood a head above him.

Royss chuckled. "Yes, Runith is new, but he is no Gorger. He's the Beastling." Yeila nodded. Had she been brought here by an unexplained invitation? He turned to Runith. "Gorgers have the strength of a giant and the wit of a scholar. She is here in case you are unable to successfully control any of the beasts."

Royss placed a delicate hand–uncommon from him–on the robed woman's shoulder. "This is Horrah, an apothecary and alchemist, here to heal you and Yeila, should an accident occur."

Kael took a trebling step back. Noticing the boy's hesitance, Runith straightened his shoulders. *Teach him well.* "I should have assumed, with someone like me in your employment." His palms were sweating, and he feared a quiver would show in his voice. Humor seemed an ever-reliable solace. "Is the Seer going to test me in a knife fight? I don't want to disfigure his face any worse than it already is."

Thraen opened his mouth in a wide sneer. He began to spit retorts from his too-perfect teeth until Royss caught the group's attention with a feigned laugh.

"No," began Royss. "He was the one who procured the beast for the first official test of your ability. Yeila will provide strength and force if your newfound powers are insufficient. Let us begin with a bird, then move on to a more *hazardous* opponent. For that one, I suggest Kael follow me and the other non-Endowed to a safe distance. Clear, Runith?"

"I'm sure I can figure it out. Where's the bird?"

Royss smirked. "That is for you to tell me. There are enough trees around, and I hear plenty of chirping.

Prove your tracking skills. Surely birds are no challenge compared to zeins. Show us your prowess, Runith the hunter!"

Runith chuckled. *Does he truly expect this of me? No instruction? No example? Perd him. Perd me.*

He left the group to pace about the courtyard with an upturned ear. Some birds called from the west, but a stronger chorus sang from a tree just beyond the jousting stand. Eager eyes followed him and he beckoned them forward and around the empty seating.

Royss glared at him. Confident or demeaning, he could not tell. Kael watched, offering a timid nod. Runith had no son, but he felt as if Kael looked up to him as a father. He would never boast that he was an ideal role-model, but he often corrected himself to help Kael become something of worth. He returned the nod, brightening Kael's now eager grin.

"Chee! Chee!" *No, that's off.* "Peet! Peet! Peet!" Runith continued on with a variety of attempts, only yielding a laugh from Royss.

"Sorry, Runith, but those are noises I never expected to hear from you. Maybe it's more than just making sounds. Listen to them. Give it time. We'll be here."

Runith took in another steady breath, trying to hide his shame from the apothecary and her polite, yet amiable, smile. She grinned, not in disappointment, but with hope, as if offering a soft embrace.

He stepped closer to the tree, glaring up through the labyrinth of branches, noticing small flickers of movement.

He felt as if his ears were now clear, like eyes wiped from water after a swim.

The choir became distinct voices, some higher in the trees, some to the right, each with their own unique tone. Their frequency differentiated, revealing their individual desires. Some invited others to join them, some warned of danger, while others called for a mate. Their vocalization rang in his ears and down his throat, strumming his vocal cords. His throat began to flex. He understood the language of birds as if he had joined their flock.

He called with an outstretched neck, mirroring the call of the birds above. Like a plume of smoke from above the tree, the flock swirled in a cloud and descended to surround Runith.

The observers stepped back in astonishment, then cheered.

He thanked and dismissed the flock and called out with a new tone, summoning a different flock of crows from a neighboring tree. As they landed in a dense circle around him, Runith conversed with them like old friends.

He chortled, cawing for another minute before dismissing them to their tree. With a jovial visage, he returned Royss with genuine confidence, one that need not be falsified to suit his ego.

"Well, then," began Royss, "it seems to work. How does it feel?"

"*Exhilarating*. I expected the initial difficulty, but once I began, it was as natural as speaking with you. It was as if I were speaking in the common tongue, yet there was a slight change." He paused. "It was like speaking to a southern Zhaesman in his dialect.."

Royss nodded. "Ready for the next step?"

"It cannot be much more difficult. What will it be this time?"

Royss turned to Thraen with an inquisitive brow.

The Seer stepped forward, smiling with a sadistic demeanor. "Tell me, *Runith*, have you ever encountered a *buyak* on one of your jolly hunts?"

He shook his head. "Never heard of them."

"They are of Gruth origin, preferring the seaside climate, but our humid lakes and bogs suffice. We were fortunate enough to procure one for... our organization's purposes."

What purposes could criminals have for beasts? Did they already have a Beastling among them? He felt it smart to not probe further.

"Yeila," Royss tossed a chain of long keys to the Gorger, "set it free."

She caught them without breaking eye contact and walked towards a barred tunnel near the west end of the field. Runith failed to notice the supposed cage earlier, dismissing it as a sewage tunnel. Royss guided the others back and up to glare over from the back of the top row of seats as Runith joined Yeila at her side.

She unlatched the lock, dropping it to the floor and lifting a horizontal bar the size of her arms.

Slaps on dank stone echoed from deep within the tunnel. Runith could not see any movement, but intermittent hissing grew in volume as he drew closer.

Yeila held the gate closed and checked back for Runith. She waved him away and he stepped back, leaving a tree's length between him and the tunnel. He responded with another nod and she pulled the gate open. It swung wide, and she jumped atop the large tunnel with a superhuman pounce, crouching to wait and see if her aid would be necessary.

The slaps across the tunnel grew closer. Light reflected from black eyes within, the shade still obscuring the lurking figure.

An unholy combination of a viper's hiss and a child's scream echoed from the chamber. Thraen's buyak sprinted from its hiding place and towards Runith.

What came forth appeared to be a hairless wolf with red, veiny skin. Its snout was as long as a stork's beak. Three appendages as long as the snout protruded from the sides of its face like thick tails, not unlike tentacles, reminiscent of a vulpine axolotl.

He forgot himself and fell to the ground as the creature pursued him. He listened as frightened prey, rather than as a Beastling. Mere moments remained until its long-taloned paws reached him. *Listen. Think. Peace.*

As if time slowed, he felt the creature's vibrations in his ears, echoing in his mind.

He lifted a hand to stop the creature, though it would provide no protection. *Dismiss human instinct, embrace animal instinct.*

Yeila jumped onto the floor and ran after the buyak.

Runith held his breath, focusing on the vibrations. Vibrations became sounds. Sounds became emotions, then thoughts.

"Stop. I'm no enemy." He spoke but knew that the others would only hear the creature's wail shouted from his mouth.

The buyak fell back, spreading its legs with a glare.

Trust me, I would feel just as weird if you spoke to me in my tongue, he thought as he stood. *"Come here. I want to speak."*

It approached him. It did not seem afraid of being spoken to by a human, but more so by the circumstances. *Poor thing must have been frightened by captivity. Poor thing? Since when did I care?*

"Why have you taken me? I want the sea," the buyak asked.

"I'm sure you will return soon enough."

"I want the sea. I want fish. I want the sea."

The creature did not seem as bright as the crows, who had spoken as philosophers. In comparison, the buyak seemed like a starved beggar, abducted from its home, and forced into unnatural circumstances.

"I can try to–"

"I want the sea! Take me back!" Its anger grew, and it turned to Yeila, eyeing her with a predatory glare.

"No!" Runith wailed. Yeila covered her ears, and the buyak turned away from her, cowering.

"Listen to me. I will find a way to help you. Please listen."

"Please help," its voice sank into despair. Its fleshy face tendrils fell low like a whimpering hound's tail. *"Skin dry, need the sea."*

Its skin was moist and shiny in certain skin folds, but cracks were noticeable along its snout and on the tops of its paws. Its face tentacles seemed to move with lethargy, some bled from dry patches.

Our lakes and bogs suffice? You perding Seer. It needs to return to Gruth.

"Calm yourself. You will return, I swear."

"Humans, empty promises."

Does it understand humans, or has it been treated poorly by other Beastlings? Unlikely.

"I will be better than them. I like that man as much as you do." He shot a quick glare at Thraen.

The buyak did not nod, for that was too human a gesture. It turned its head from side to side, hissing. Not only could Runith learn their languages, but he had also been able to adapt to some of their customs and mannerisms. *Thank Laeih for this gift.*

"Ready to lock it back up, Runith?" Royss called from atop the stands. "It seems like you have tamed it well enough."

"I think—" *Hold the justice. Best not cause any contention with the Seer, it would only make the buyak's captivity worse.*

He turned to give a final reassurance. *"Return to the tunnel. I will find a way out. I promise."* It paused and replied with a hiss. He returned the gesture.

"Yeah, send it back." *Repress sorrow, show confidence.* "I think I've shown the kulf what I am capable of."

Yeila closed the tunnel's gate as the buyak retreated into its depths. As Royss and the other two descended the stands, Runith glared back into the tunnel with solemnity and a promise.

Kael was more jovial than he had ever seen. Royss feigned professionalism, though he seeped with excitement like a Chussman seeing the sea for the first time.

Thraen offered a nod, which Runith returned with minimal eye contact.

"You seem competent enough. Now let us discuss some *productive* uses of your skills, rather than these tavern tricks." Royss turned to the others. "Thank you all for your service. You are free to leave. Runith, follow me back into the Canton. Kael is welcome to join." The others bid farewell, and Kael walked timidly at Royss' side.

Runith paced in silence. He was astounded at the empathy he felt for the buyak. He had faced creatures that spoke as any human, yet he had no problem killing them for a bounty. Beasts are not human, yet he felt something within, challenging that long-held bias. *Did I hunt before for the thrill of slaying, or for the payment?* The buyak had shown him that these so-called beasts were not mere abominations, but living beings. *What other creatures have I unjustly slain for the convenience of one willing to pay?*

CHAPTER FOUR

LET US BEGIN

"Why did you employ a perding Bronze Seer?" asked Runtih as Kael shut the door to Royss' study chamber. Runith rested in his usual seat but edged toward the front edge.

"I needed something more fearsome than birds. Tell me, Runith, where else would I capture something as vile as a buyak?"

Runith capitulated to a reluctant nod. Kael imitated him as he sat at his side.

"The Seers are not the lawbreakers that the public believe them to be. Demeaning them to the office of a petty thief is as simpleminded as seeing all Priessmen as hedonists. Trust me, I am no lover of Priesssmen, but we too often see them all as villains. Thraen is not the most amiable among my business associates, but he has helped the Canton of Agriculture more than most sanctimonious Zhaesmen. Do not forget that he too is a Zhaesmen. We all have our sins. The seers only choose to express them in a different manner."

"If you claim to know them so well, what do the Bronze Seers accomplish besides debauchery and thievery?"

"That is not mine to divulge." Royss offered a wink to brush it off, but Runith would not succumb to credulity so easily. He trusted Royss but could not deny that he felt uneasy about his camaraderie with racketeers. "I apologize if Thraen's presence bothered you, but you can't complain about Yeila. You're no Gorger, but I have no doubt you could win her over."

"Actually, I was more impressed by the apothecary."

"Horrah? Truly? Well, perhaps I could find an opportunity for you two to work together." Royss chuckled. "It's a rare sight to see you blush, Runith. Enough of that though, let us put those abilities to work. Ready for your first *new* hunt?"

Runith paused, clearing his boyish mind from dwelling on Horrah. "I suppose so. What will it be this time?"

"Have you ever been to the Cloven Gleff?"

Kael's eyes bounced back and forth between Runith and Royss during their conversation. He did not seem bothered by their ignorance of his presence, rather he sat as an interested spectator.

"I know I look rough enough to be a miner, but no."

"You will know it soon enough. We have called you and given you the gift of an Endowed organ so that you can serve the Court and its needs. A recent chain of disturbances has caused material losses and even some deaths in the Gleff's tunnels. Some of our most valuable passages deep within the mine have collapsed."

"There is a reason only for the desperate work there. Aren't these typical occurrences? Breaking rocks all day is bound to cause some to fall."

Royss shook his head, pulling a map out from a drawer beneath his desk. "They happen, but not daily, as these have over the past few weeks." He unrolled a map of the Gleff's tunnels and waved his hand over the left side. "All of these passages have been evacuated and mining therefore halted. They assumed this would resolve the trouble, which it did for a time, but the occurrences began once again here, here, and here." He pointed to the three largest tunnels on the right side. Two of them had circular camps drawn in the middle of each tunnel.

"Have the laborers seen anything?"

"Of course. Why else would I send you? Some have survived to tell of an insidious beast, though their stories may be exaggerated. They are miners, after all."

Runith stared at him, impatient with his chauvinism. "Yes, and..."

Kael's left buttock fell off of his seat, causing him to stumble back into his chair in embarrassment.

Runith chuckled. The boy could act like a sober adult when needed, but he often fell into childish wonderment. Maybe Runith could learn something from that. There is a balance to all pleasures in life.

"Like I said, these are miners, many of whom would concoct a tale to have a day off of work. I assume those who stayed too long to catch a glimpse of the creature perished in its wake, while those who only took a brief look focused on escape more than preparing a tale for taverns. The descriptions range from giant moles, imps with claws as long as a man. Some claim they saw a kaesan, though I doubt that."

"What do they want there? Did someone send them? Chussmen or Priessmen? Do they think the beasts eat bronze?"

Royss grinned with a smirk. "That, Runith, is for you to find out."

"But I am no investigator. I'm a foolish beastslayer!"

"You are not foolish, sir!" retorted Kael.

"The boy is right," added Royss. "I would never have chosen you if you did not have something in your head. Remember, you are a Beast*caller* now, not a slayer."

"So you want me to keep the thing alive when I find it?"

Royss nodded. "If we want to avoid this happening in the future, we need to study it."

He hated to show hesitancy to Royss, and especially to Kael. He was a guard. The perding *captain* of Royss' guard. Was this some twisted punishment for his impulsive hunts? Kael offered a hopeful grin, one that helped soothe his worries.

"We will not send you alone. I can ask Yeila to join, maybe with another Gorger. Horrah would travel under your *protection.*"

Runith opened his mouth with a retort on the edge of his tongue, but surrendered to a chuckle and shook his head. "Perd me. When do you want me to leave?"

"Are you ready, Kael?" Royss asked.

"I su...suppose I am."

"Great! I will have a carriage prepared to leave from the Canton at dawn."

Runith wanted to argue but submitted to the request of his superior. What had he expected when chosen to become one of these "*blessed Endowed*?" Runith was the type of man to boast of his hunts to the whole tavern. He would have Gorger companions and a healer, yet he felt apprehensive this time. What had happened to him? He could control beasts with ease, or at least he had so far. Was Laeih warning him with guardian spirits, or was it that lingering visage of the Bronze Scholar that dug under his skin? Regardless, his tongue was dry despite the humidity, and could only be soothed with enough mead to put him to sleep.

CHAPTER FIVE

THE CLOVEN GLEFF

M orning had come with its clarion call. Kael joined Runith to walk down the cobbled streets of central Kzhek to meet with the other members of the company. They both lived in the heart of the city. It was no mere coincidence that they found each other before reaching the Canton of Agriculture. Though Kael seemed anxious, Runith would not be surprised to find that the boy had waited for him on the street all night.

The morning mist had not yet cleared, obscuring their way. Runith was born and raised in Kzhek; he could navigate it blind. Kael followed him like a lost child, having spent most of his life in eastern Zhaes near the border. So far, the boy hadn't shown any Priess influence in his demeanor, much to his benefit.

Figures grew clearer. Two large reptilian cats without ears, Ghete, stood before a carriage in their bridles. Royss began to clap and cheer as they approached. Runith appreciated the comedic gesture but was not as accustomed to early hours as the Thane seemed to be. Yeila grimaced and stared at the Thane with antagonism. He was glad to see that he was not the only one that had already reached his limit of Royss for a while. He admired the Thane and counted him among his closest friends, but even a rambunctious brute needed some time away from Royss' personality.

"Seems like we are all here!" Royss exclaimed.

"You're coming?" Runith scratched his baggy eyes.

"No, merely bidding you farewell. Do you need anything else for the journey?"

"Food." said a large Zhaesmen to Yeila's side, likely another Gorger.

"We have plenty loaded in the back of the carriage, Rhen, though the mining camps near the Gleff will have more if you need it. I had two days' worth of food for each of you prepared, not ignoring the fact that the Endowed need twice the amount to eat. I hope that you will not be there longer than that. You should arrive within the hour with these ghete, for those unfamiliar with the distance. I recognize that it is not a distant journey, but I hope to repay you in comfort for your service."

"Only comfort?" Yeila asked, a groggy tone still lingering from an early morning.

"We're not Sleffmen," Royss chuckled. "You can collect your pay after your return. This is the best use of taxes that I've heard of in a while, though I may request funding for a new statue in my hall. Enough of me. Off you go."

Runith stood in the back of the line while the others entered the carriage. Royss spectated on the side, giving self-satisfied nods.

"I am confident in you, Runith. You've already proven yourself."

He bid Royss one last farewell with the Zhaes salute, repeating the Zhaes Ideal. "Whole is the Holy, Thane Belik."

"Whole is the Holy, Beastling."

⊱⋆⊰

Kael fell asleep and slid onto Runith's shoulder near the end of the ride. He admired the boy as a son but would not treat him as a child. He pushed Kael away, relieved that the boy's snores continued. Kael spent the rest of the ride asleep, never awakening to his head slamming against the side of the carriage as the carriage crossed a rocky terrain.

The trail grew progressively more rugged as they neared the base camp of the Cloven Gleff. Noting the unpaved trail, Runith understood why the lower-class workers were increasingly furious over the nobility's use of their taxes.

Through the window he saw laborers preparing their gear for the day's labors. It was cruel irony that Zhaes prided itself on its bronze from the Gleff, yet they treated those who mined it worse than a grimy residue after a rainstorm. The world was filled with injustices, yet he would not overwhelm himself. If each person cleansed an illness from society, the realms of men would be holier. Beasts were his responsibility. That was sufficient for the time being.

Runith felt as if he still shook from the terrain after the carriage stopped. Yeila and Rhen–Runith had to ask a few times to remember the second Gorger's name–exited the carriage first, followed by Kael, Horrah, and finally, Runith.

"Who do we talk to? I'm ready to go!" Runith said, shaking his legs loose.

Horrah turned to him. "Yeila is leading. Royss gave her directions and a name before you arrived." She did not seem intimidated or bothered by his personality, but it would likely take some time for him to grow on her.

"Right, right. I suppose that one is my fault."

"Your fault?" She turned to him with a grin. "Who said you were the one to lead?"

"Well... I suppose that—"

"Prove yourself in the caverns, *Beastling*." She smirked as she turned her focus ahead.

They paced up a hill and through the mining camp's dirt streets. Mud clung to his feet with the morning moisture, though it did not seem as though it had rained. Smells of cured meat and stewing oats caught them as they passed by small fires. Though Zhaesmen avoided overly salted meats, they had to rely on foods that would last while on duty. Unless these miners had a lucky evening, it would be a long while until they tasted the soft white fish so cherished in Kzhek. Runith's stomach called for him to join them, but Yeila walked at a too-determined pace. He hadn't spoken more than a few sentences with her, yet her actions spoke of her personality.

Kael fell behind. He seemed to have had too little rest.

Runith let Horrah catch the Gorgers, while he held back to place his arm on Kael's shoulder. "Are you able to hold up?"

"Yes...yes, sir. Don't fret over me, you're the one who needs to speak with a creature from the under realms."

"You don't think," Runith's scowl grew tense, "that these are beasts from the under realms, do you?"

Kael chuckled, each laugh less joyous than the previous.

"No, I'm serious, Kael. What if the tunnels of the Gleff connect to the under realms, and demonic dwellers are the source of the havoc?"

"You, sir, are as gullible as a Sleffman sometimes, but I do not mean to offend."

"You should. Slandering me would build your character. Don't worry, Kael, my emotions are hidden far too deep. Maybe they've fallen into the under realms."

"I think the under realms are more of an off-world plane, rather than something in our world."

Runith nodded.

Kael looked uncomfortable in the silence and broke it before it made him sweat any more than he already was. "You know, I don't think you are as cold as you claim to be."

"What do you mean?"

"I've seen more than the bloodthirsty hunter in you. Don't worry, I won't ruin your hard-earned reputation."

"You know, Kael, even as I approach my forty-second year, I still am trying to learn who I am. I thought I was a mere guard, but it seems that Laeih has more in hand for me."

"The gods work wonders for those who surrender themselves to their will."

He looked away from the boy's hopeful smile to see Yeila holding the door flap open for them to enter the largest yurt in sight.

Runith described himself as a Zhaesman with a rough appearance, but the man seated in the back of the yurt made him feel like a nobleman. A woman and another man stood at his sides, peering over his shoulders at a roll of parchment on a table.

"What large Zhaesmen!" he shouted. "You must be the Gorgers and that one back there"—he pointed at Kael—"must be the Beastling Royss told me of!"

"Actually, I–"

"That would be me," Runith raised a hand.

"I would have guessed you were a Gorger as well, despite being smaller than the other two. Very well," he stood to greet the party. "My name is Tholn, Proctor of Zhaes ore. These two are the miners that you will be working with. Best not tell you their names. You would forget them before you enter the tunnels." He chuckled.

The name sounded familiar, but Runith would have remembered the man if he had seen him before. Though he worked directly under Royss as one of the Proctors to the Canton of Agriculture, he must spend all his time in his field of labor. Runith would have never guessed that this man was a nobleman, but he appreciated any leader who worked at their inferiors' sides.

Yeila introduced the group, and Tholn invited them forward with welcoming arms. Kael wiped his fogged spectacles as he glared from behind Runith at the center of the crowded table.

"As I am sure Royss informed you," Tholn pointed at the oil-stained map, "most of our assaults have been in this sector of the mine. We have since pulled out our efforts there, hoping to avoid any further complications, but the nuisance is now in our eastern tunnels as well. We can only hope that it is a single beast that has since tunneled across. Laeih help us if we have to deal with two of those things. A man can only hope that Royss' *prized* Beastling can help cure us of this."

"One creature seems simple enough," boasted Runith. Tholn seemed to be lacking in confidence. Someone had to fulfill the role.

Tholn scratched his balding pate with an anxious laugh. "If only it were so. Crevice imps have filled the abandoned tunnels. We usually do well without any infestations but leaving these sectors without miners for a few weeks now has invited unwanted guests."

"Maybe we could use them to help us with the larger problem," Runith said. "I've called flocks of birds at once. I don't think numbers will be a problem."

Tholn shook his head. "Royss may want you to keep the big one alive for his personal interests, but I want the crevice imps out of my tunnels. Sure, use a few if you must, but eradicate them when you finish. Once you leave, I doubt your beast-charming abilities will keep them under control from a distance. It looks like your Gorgers each have a claymore. If I wasn't clear enough, the Beastling can control the big beast, and the Gorgers can kill anything in the way."

"Are the imps combative? What if they are no more than fish in a pond, searching for shelter?" Runith tried to remain firm in his voice but failed to do so. *I had no problem slaying an entire population of zeins a few weeks ago. What makes this any different? What is happening to you, you perding kulf? Did this organ turn you into some sympathetic Chussman? Are you going to weep over plucked grass next?*

"They steal anything we leave and have killed a couple of my miners this week. Perd, even their feces make the caverns unbearable. A couple of my miners said the stench made them sick for a week. Could have just been some lazy ones, who knows? Nevertheless, I want them out of there."

"We will see it taken care of, sir," Yeila said with an overly firm voice.

"I appreciate the help." He gave a beaten-down grin. "Well then, you can find anything you need here in camp. Food and extra clothing are at the base of the hill. I only ask that you leave the drinking until after. This mess has already cost me too many fine Zhaesmen. I don't want to lose any more, especially any of you new *Endowed*."

The title for those who received grafts sounded unnecessarily aggrandizing, but people seemed insistent on using it. *Better get used to it as you are one of them.*

"Shall we head in?" asked Runith.

"Surely we could benefit from some time to sit and strategize," offered Yeila.

"Nah," Runith shook his head. "You kill the imps and I'll talk to the master at the end of the tunnel. I'd like to sleep in my own bed tonight. Royss gave us two days, but that is a poor estimation of our talent. Why waste time?"

"Ah, well... we need to... I believe—"

Yeila stumbled for words until Kael ended her thoughtless rambling. "Sounds like a great plan, Sir Beastling."

Runith turned to him with a wink and smirk, making sure to hide it from Yeila.

Tholn stood and led the party outside. "Continue up the trail and veer left. If you want to enter the center of conflict, take the rightmost tunnel marked number four above the entrance. I expect to see one of you riding out on the back of the beast when you return." He chuckled and slapped Kael on the back as they left, causing him to stumble.

CHAPTER SIX

IMPISH

T he ascending trail stretched for half an hour of walking. Though it was not steep, it would be a tedious journey for miners frequenting this channel of caves. It proved useful in protecting the camps by providing ample distance from most of the crevice imps.

"I hear you were quite the beast hunter," Horrah mentioned as she quickened her pace to walk beside Runith.

"I suppose I was," Runith replied.

"I would hope that you still are."

"Me too." He returned to a contemplative silence. In previous hunts, his only worries were being under-compensated for the brutal killings. Today, however, payment was the last thing on his mind. Did the Gorgers worry likewise about their grafts? Had their new organs affected their minds?

Abandoned torches were fastened to each side of the cavern. The entrance opened like an ancient titan's mouth, darkness leading back into an unknown abyss. Small cracks and clatters echoed from within the chamber, though they were not the sounds of gravity pulling rocks to the floor.

"On with it." Runith pressed at the Gorger's backs.

"I am only assessing the path ahead, Beastling." Yeila sneered.

"What are you going to do, sniff it? Calculate the location of the rocks clattering within? Let me answer your questions. The imps are likely all over. You two kill them. I'll take the larger beast. Kael is already pissing himself. I'm sure their keen senses will smell it before your *strategies* are solidified. Onward, Zhaesmen."

Horrah hid a shy smirk behind a scratch of her nose. Yeila began to cough up a retort but was pressed forward with Rhen's arm reaching around her shoulders. She threw it off as if she were to cleave it free with her claymore. Runith need not ask what their relationship entailed. He chuckled at the poor fellow's hopeless pursuit.

Horrah lit two torches from her bag and passed them to Runith and Kael. "Light the torches on the walls as you pass. Make sure the Gorgers can see their enemies."

The group nodded and entered the cavern.

The blend of cavernous mold and the remains of imp feedings along the way nearly caused Runith to vomit. Mounds of torn flesh revealed broken rib cages and split deer heads were shoved into the corners, leading Runith to question if the imps were equipped with weapons.

"Is it true, sir?" Whispered Kael.

"What?" Runith replied with a tame voice, though it was no whisper.

Kael's eyes flew around the halls, fearing that they would be heard. Despite Runith's lackadaisical confidence, he continued to whisper. "I did *not* urinate in my trousers, but you said that the imps can smell it. Are their senses truly that keen?"

Runith lowered his voice. "Who knows? I just needed the Gorgers to move."

Kael remained somewhat frustrated but could not dispel his grin.

Runith had dealt with other imp races in the past and assumed that crevice imps could not be more intelligent than their relatives. Even if he tried to communicate with them, he was sure that their language would be close to that of an illiterate drunkard. They knew how to kill well enough to feed themselves and had a particular liking for valuables. Perhaps the bronze had drawn them into the mines, yet they would never be able to learn to smelt or put the ore to use. The lust of wealth traps the wisest and the dullest alike. He did not deny that he was a victim of greed in the past, but this task seemed to have a deeper meaning, one that he was yet to discover.

Yeila stopped with one hand held back and the other drawing her sword. Their conversation had distracted him, but once the silence returned, he noted that footsteps clearly slapped the ground ahead.

A cobra-like hiss followed unintelligible grunts. Three hunched imps ran into the flickering torchlight, each one half as tall as a human. Their earlobes pointed sharply downward, like dripping paint. Their faces were of a dark gray with angered wrinkles. Ragged loincloth covered their groins, while the breasts were exposed on males and females alike. They were not horribly intimidating until they revealed their needle-like teeth.

Rhen stumbled at their vile approach, dropping his blade with a clatter. More footsteps drew closer.

The first imp jumped them and Yeila cleaved it in two. She beheaded the other two while Rhen retrieved his sword. Before he stood straight, an imp fell from the cavern's ceiling.

"Get it *off!*" He wailed as the imp dug its dagger-like claws between the cracks of his armor. Runith feared that his cry caught the attention of every imp in the chamber.

Yeila impaled the imp, pulling him back while more fell from above.

Kael ran back with Horrah. Much to their relief, the cavern remained clear behind them. Runith remained a few paces behind the Gorgers and held his torch to illuminate the cavern's ceiling. At least twenty imps swarmed them with their claws dug into the rocks above. With how easily they cut through rock with their hands, he feared for Rhen's well-being.

Yeila waved for them to fall back, taking steps backward as she cut down the imps with Rhen. They seemed capable at the moment, but Rhen's strikes became more lethargic with each swing. *Perd, has he ever touched a sword?* Very few living people had. Combat was a skill honed by hunters and lost by most in ancient wars.

Runith stepped up behind Rhen, who struck down one at a time compared to Yeila's swings that slayed two or three at once. He knew Tholn wanted them to exterminate the imps, but it would do no harm to utilize them while he could. If they proved fruitless against their own, he would at least have an opportunity to refine his Beastling abilities before their ultimate goal.

Runith hissed over the sound of metal through flesh, grunting as he caught the eyes of the frontmost crevice imps. Then turned back.

"Keep your eyes forward," Runith commanded. "I'll distract some of them while you finish them off."

Rhen continued his lethargic strikes and Yeila nodded with her head facing forward.

Runith repeated the call and two imps fell still. *Can I coerce them to join us? Am I merely speaking to them or are they under my command?* The buyak seemed to obey with little trouble. Was that the situation, the creature's willingness, or another facet of a Beastling's ability? He was sure that he would learn soon enough. The consequences were dire. Rather than tread in shallow water, he dove in.

"Attack those behind you." He commanded in their squealing tongue.

His two targets remained, staring at him with an unfocused gaze.

He paused, taking the calls of the other imps into his ears as if he were a scribe, prepared to transcribe them. His pitch was too high. They seemed to hear him, but his message was unclear. They were words not yet piercing their soul.

"Attack each other." His voice penetrated like a sharpened arrow. The two imps shook their blank stares, bared their teeth, and ran towards each other. They hissed as

they punched and clawed with chaotic swipes. Portions of the imp horde joined in, but a barrage still clashed against the Gorgers.

Runith called again, trying to distract those who continued to assault the Gorgers. He was sure that he hit the right pitch, yet it did not change their determination. *Do they have a stronger will? Are they more susceptible to persuasion?*

Yeila and Rhen finished those before them and fell the remaining mob that tore at each other.

"Thank you, Beastling. I fear it would have been worse..." Rhen paused to cough bloody sputum onto the rock wall. "... it would have gone worse without your help."

Yeila offered a nod of appreciation.

"Horrah," Runith called, "come quick." Runith caught Rhen as he fell and lowered him to the cavern floor. Horrah knelt at Rhen's side, removing bottles and vials, mixing them while she handed Yeila a damp cloth. "Take your armor off," Horrah commanded. "I know it will hurt, but we need to see how deep it is."

He complied with groans as he doffed his helm and the plating around his torso. "I...it's...it's hard to breathe. Wh... what should I...do?"

Horrah removed her tight black glove and pressed her bare palm to his back. "This is going to take more than a quick salve."

"What do you mean?" asked Runith. He stepped closer to Horrah to look at the injury in the Gorger's thickly muscled back. Four distinct claw marks traced diagonally across his back, each one digging deeper than the last. The rightmost claw left no more than a painful scratch, while the leftmost claw only left a hole the size of an eye.

"Will he live?" he whispered into her ear; no one else seemed to hear him over Rhen's panting.

"He should," Horrah shook a small vial of light blue liquid with one hand while the other remained on his back. "You are going to feel some tightness in your chest, Rhen." She shook the vial, capping the opening with her finger, then poured the liquid into the hole as quickly as possible.

Rhen inhaled with a wide mouth, gasping as if he had just arisen from underwater. He coughed large clumps of dark-red mucus out, clenching his fists as he caught his breath.

"What in Laeih's name was that?" Runith was astounded. He had seen people wounded like that from past hunts. That was the type of injury that caused one to resign all hopes of survival.

"Wipe the wound, Yeila." Horrah moved to the side, still keeping her palm against Rhen's back.

"Horrah! What was—"

"Quiet, Beastling. I have no doubt that there are more imps deeper in the cavern." She sighed, annoyed. "I try to use these abilities as little as possible with all the controversy over grafting. I'm an Eurythrin if that wasn't clear by my touch."

Horrah stood and left Yeila to keep pressure on the wound with a new rag dampened by a yellow elixir. Horrah wiped her hands with some water from her sack and donned her gloves once again. "He had a punctured lung. It collapsed and would have caused respiratory failure if I hadn't stopped his blood and given him that vial of brethyl."

Runith stared, his mind frozen with shock.

"What is that?" Kael asked.

"Brethyl is an elixir commonly given to miners who suffer from the fumes that remain in the caverns from long days of mining. It's made from some northern herbs, but that is beyond your concern. It soothes an air-starved body and, as I assumed, helped restore Rhen's breathing. I manipulated some of his inner humors and re-closed the lung, among some other repairs to keep him breathing. He will be sore for a few days but should be able to breathe as usual. I did not plan on using that elixir but figured it would be useful if we were trapped somehow. Pray that we will not need anymore, because I would only have enough for three of us."

Runith had brushed off his ignorance of the Endowed revolution when Royss called him to become a Beastling, yet he felt more embarrassed this time. Life as a Canton guard was simple enough, but now, his life entailed a more complex story. He was no scholar, nor would he claim to be, but he thought himself intelligent enough for a common Zhaesman. If he were to survive this new epoch of divinely gifted beings, he would have to better educate himself for the coming days.

Yeila helped Rhen back to his feet after his wound was bandaged and his armor, once again, donned. His breath returned, though he hissed at the initial pain of recovering.

"Are you able to keep going, Zhaesman?" asked Runith, with a light hand on his shoulder.

"Yeah," he laughed, "I wouldn't say that I was afraid of some fighting, but I would have swung my sword free of inhibitions if I had known she was an Eurythrin!"

"That is the very reason why I keep that trait hidden. People who battle recklessly are bound to kill themselves and their allies. I cannot fix every problem, I hope you know that. If those claws pierced a little to the left, your heart would have been struck, and that is beyond my prowess."

Rhen turned his head, trying to scratch away his embarrassment and returning anxiety.

"Are you medicinally trained?" Yeila asked.

Had she spoken anything other than a command during the entire journey? She waved the group forward, not wanting to waste more time standing and conversing.

"Nothing more than reading, more skimming, some tomes on the basics of healing. Eurythrins, as far as I have experienced, have a sixth sense. We use the sense to feel the rhythm and flow of our body or that of another. While I can survive a sword through my stomach, I can just as well stop an amputated arm from bleeding."

"Surely, Royss knows of your ability?" Runith asked.

"No, he sent an herbal witch to accompany you."

He stared.

"I jest, though it is unwise to doubt herbal remedies. The Thanes of the Court are aware of my prowess and unique ability as an Endowed, *but*, as I said before, I like to keep that private. Political strife has settled in the year since harvesting was implemented, but the Chussmen and Tchoyasmen are still very much opposed to the process. I like to make as few enemies as I can, regardless of my identity."

He felt the need to argue but felt no words could rebut her sincerity. The party nodded and continued onward.

Runith had to relight his torch from Kael's flame to continue lighting the path. It seemed as if twenty minutes had passed, yet no sound suggested the presence of crevice imps. Had they all been killed in the first tunnels of their exploration? He doubted it would be that easy.

The caverns grew wider, changing from a small corridor to a grand hall, and split more frequently. The map seemed simple enough to follow and their path had not yet disproved the correctness of their journey.

"How's the battle-wound, Gorger?" Runith broke the long-still silence, hoping to invite an emotion besides fear.

"My cough has dissipated, though I feel like I drank a shot of a Gruth spirit. My chest burns, but I'm alive. That is sufficient for now."

"Then grab your sword!" commanded Yeila. Wet gnashing from a brutal feast came into light. Runith waved Horrah and Kael back and stepped right behind the Gorgers.

Before them and under the light from Runith's torch, five cavern imps tore at a sickly corpse. He would not claim proficiency in aging corpses, but this one appeared to be no more than a few days old.

Two continued to tear at the victim's innards, hypnotized by bloodlust. The other three bared their teeth like white stiletto knives dipped in red paint and ran towards the Gorgers.

Five would be no difficult feat, especially noting that two of them were oblivious to their new guests. Yeila decapitated one and impaled the other. Rhen downed another with a swing that cut from the crown of the imp's head until it lost momentum in its abdomen.

Rhen's strike seemed lackadaisical, yet it proved more than useful. *How weak were the imps' bodies?* One did not expect much else from creatures that feasted on waste. Yeila stepped ahead to behead the final two as Rhen basked in the carnage of his brutal trophy.

"Is that a Chussman?" Yeila asked.

Runith scowled. "I haven't seen many Chussmen miners in our Court. Maybe some Sleffmen, but rarely anyone from Court Chuss."

She waved them over to peer at the corpse. Kael held to the opposite wall, squeezing his eyes closed with dry heaves..

"He's not wearing mining gear." Yeila lifted the head by its hood.

"Dark skin and dressed for the desert. By Laeih, that *is* a Chussman." Runith stood with hands on his hips. "That is no miner, nor any lowly laborer. Look at that golden sash. I would be willing to gamble that this man works in a Chuss Canton for some Thane."

"But why would he be here, dressed like that?" asked Rhen. He kept his distance but was not as hesitant as Kael to conduct his inspection.

"Noblemen are always oblivious to the physical requirements of labor outside a Canton. Unless he was an Endowed, it was his own foolishness that killed him." Runith said.

Yeila turned back to face him. "Chussmen oppose grafting. The only person from Court Chuss that would have an ability would be a natural-born Endower. I would not say this man is five years old."

"What would a Chussman want in the Zhaes mines?" asked Rhen.

Runith shook his head and drew an unsteady scowl. "Zhaes power and influence comes from the fruits of this mine. I would hope that this is no hint of war."

"Unlikely," Yeila did not give a moment to contemplate the possibility. "War has not occurred in centuries and is a barbaric waste of life. I would assume that this man had some criminal ties, hoping to benefit from our labors. Chussmen claim love for others, *'Care is the Creed,'* as their ideal states, but that does not discount the inevitability of sinners. No Zhaesmen is perfect in obedience either."

Ah yes, holy philosophy. I bask at your righteousness. Runith scratched his lips to hide his smile. "Do you think there are more?"

Yeila shrugged. "I suppose we shall find out."

CHAPTER SEVEN

PRAISE THE MOLE

Rumbles and distant cracks echoed like the amplified crawling of the crevice imps. They were nearing the farthest reaches of the map's left tunnels; it was only appropriate that the greatest danger would await them at the end.

"You're sure that's it?" Rhen whispered.

"Does that sound like more imps to you? Perhaps Chussmen? I can't hear any prideful boasts or hypocritical complaints, so I would say it is safe to assume there are no bureaucrats."

Rhen offered a nervous laugh, suppressing it beside Runith's careless volume.

He was relieved to see that Rhen turned to him for advice. Yeila was experienced, or so she wanted them to believe, but a soldier's mindset is too thick for sound leadership. Nevertheless, she still took any opportunity to dictate their moves.

"Let's pause here and assure that we are prepared for what lies ahead." Yeila spoke louder than Rhen but was too hesitant to match Runith.

He wanted to oppose her second attempt at convening to plan but felt this one appropriate. He was the key component to taming. The Gorgers were only part of the company to support and slay any imps that tried to interfere. He hoped to Laeih that they had cleared them out by now. The cacophony of their first encounter made his speaking with the imps difficult enough. He could not imagine trying to console a titan if more imps ran about to drown his calls.

"As before," Runith began, "we will have the Gorgers lead us to any remaining imps, should we stumble upon them. Our previous formation was ideal. I will remain a few steps behind and draw closer to the beast if I need to." He wanted to give Rhen an opportunity to outshine his companion, but this was not the time for demeaning his stronger ally. "Yeila, I want you at my side as if I was the Krall of Zhaes. I need to focus on the beast's call and cannot worry about protecting myself."

She nodded. All jests were replaced with dry sobriety.

He turned to each of them, reading their eyes and offering an assuring nod to Kael who played with the bands around his wrists. "Forward?"

They nodded.

Yeila fixed her shoulders with the posture to rival a Zhaes priest. Rhen attempted to mirror her but was left lopsided as he leaned toward his wound. He turned over his shoulder to see Kael with a stance not unlike theirs. The boy had grown over their time hunting together. He only hoped that Kael's confidence was genuine this time rather than an illusion to impress the party.

Rather than a gradual expansion of the walls, the cave opened to a capacious chamber, as if they had passed through an invisible door to the beast's lair. Large scratch marks that suggested hands the size of a Zhaes-man had torn the cavern walls. Large holes as wide as a carriage opened high up on the walls. Mounds of rubble scattered throughout the chamber, with ramps of stone rising and falling along the walls. Imp corpses piled in corners and dark blood stains splattered the walls like a failed attempt at art. The far reaches of the chamber remained in darkness under Runith's single torch, but there was no hint at a hidden presence. It was the exact image one would picture for a devilish lair, yet it lacked its namesake. No creature was in sight, yet muffled rumbles continued, seemingly beyond the walls.

Runith turned back to Horrah and Kael who remained in the tunnel before the chamber's entrance. He shrugged and turned to the Gorgers who held equally puzzled glares.

Horrah took a few steps towards them but was briskly halted by Runith's forbidding palm. The thunderous rumbling grew louder, yet a veil still seemed to hide them.

The Gorger's eyes shot to the right wall. Runith followed as subsequent blasts shook loose stones from the walls.

An eruption of stone shot through the chamber as a behemoth burst through a newly formed hole to accompany its dilapidated collection.

Its head twitched as if it were a blind man searching for a calling voice.

"P... perd me," uttered Rhen. The creature's black eyes shot towards the party with a vile grimace.

Its mouth opened with the jowls of a toothed lizard to match its multi-layered neck frill, but its general appearance was more mammalian. It was reminiscent of a mole, though it was much slimmer and had a longer snout. It towered over them with its star-nose that bore long tentacles, reminding Runith of the buyak's mane. The beast crouched back on its hind legs and pounced forward to extend its long, spear-length claws. If a cavern imp and a mammoth-sized mole had a bastard child, this would be the insidious result.

Before Runith had a moment to focus on its voice, the mole seized Yeila and tossed her across the cavern.

"Runith!" Rhen cried out with a whimper. "Speak to it! I'm–"

The mole imp backhanded Rhen, merely knocking him over rather than throwing him against the wall.

"I'm trying!" *Listen, you perding kulf!* He shook his head and stared into the gnarled face that threatened to devour him.

"Gaaaaaaah!" he shouted, hoping to gain any reply from the mole imp.

It hissed, though it was not long enough for him to grasp what it was saying. To understand its call, he needed it to wail.

His eyes shot to the floor. Rhen had dropped his blade as he was hit as limp meat.

The mole imp pressed back on its heels, preparing for another spring loaded pounce.

Runith was no Gorger, but he *was* an experienced beast slayer. He did not plan on killing this time, but he needed to do something effective.

Simultaneously, he jumped and rolled towards Rhen's blade as claws shredded the air where he stood.

He rose with the blade and cut a shallow, yet precise wound in the inner fold of the creature's thigh.

A screeching groan that would leave his ears injured emanated from the angered jaws of the mole imp.

Runith jumped back and rolled behind a rock pillar, focusing as much as he could on the frequency of its cry.

He peeked out, preparing to replicate the call. No longer searching for him, the creature ran towards the closest targets. His heart thumped as the mole imp ran towards Horrah and Kael at the entrance of the cavern. There was no time to prepare, only to offer a risk, a gamble.

Runith let loose a deafening scream, straining his throat.

The mole imp stumbled, slamming into the wall beside the entrance. Rocks fell as it let out a painful wail.

He repeated the call, but it did not turn to hear him as the other beasts had. It shook on crouched legs and buried its head in its arms as if it was having an agonizing headache.

"Listen to me!" he commanded, now feeling that he hit its frequency. *"Listen! Obey! Stop! Listen!"* He barraged it with shouts. The mole imp shook like a hallucinating vagrant after ingesting a mandrake elixir. He was certain that it heard him, yet did not believe that the message penetrated deep enough. He mustered more shouts as

the beast settled, but he was taken aback as screeches came from another source.

"Runith! The tunnel!"

"What?"

Rhen pointed to the tunnel whence the beast came. He expected another mole imp but was surprised to see a small child with dark skin standing in the mouth of the hole.

A Chussboy?

The boy screeched with the sound of the mole imp. It turned its head in weak obedience. *An Endower Beast-ling. A natural-born Beastling.*

Runith called back, sending the beast into a frenzy as it was commanded by opposing voices. He spun frantically in search of a solution. Rhen limped to hide, but Yeila stood and walked alongside the cave's perimeter.

Runith ran to Yeila, still calling to the mole imp to keep it distracted.

Blood dripped from the right side of Yeila's face, rock-torn flesh matching her dented armament and torn leathers. This was no time to focus on wounds. Delaying an attack would only increase the number of injuries.

"I need to take out the Chussboy." He covered her ears and let out another call. She replied with a puzzled scowl. He turned her head and pointed to the tunnel, where the boy still stood in a vocal battle with him. She nodded and removed her crossbow from her shoulders. It was small and not designed for large hunts, but if she was a decent aim, it would serve its purpose.

Runith ran with her, hiding behind pillars and rocks along the way, and pressed her forward while he ran to the left. His call distracted not only the beast, but the boy as well, who threw rocks at Runith to no avail.

"Now!" Runith shouted. As soon as he heard the crossbow loose, he let out another call, hoping there would be no second one to contest his control. The mole imp relaxed to stare at him.

"Grab the boy." He rubbed his gloved fingers together in brisk repetition.

Please allow this grace, Laeih.

It complied with slow movements and reached toward the boy.

"Delicately." He commanded, not knowing if the boy was still alive. He felt a sinner's sting for commanding Yeila to down him. Runith held a prayer that Yeila had not taken a lethal shot.

A moan. The boy moaned as he was lifted, whimpering over his loss. The boy surrendered control of the beast as the threat of death became tangible. Children make poor loyalists. Was that not the very reason for which Endowers' organs are harvested for the benefit of society?

The boy would need aid if his wound was enough to inspire surrender. *"Take him to the entrance."*

The mole imp turned and met Horrah and Kael as Runith ran to join them.

"Lower him." It compiled. *The more they resist, the harder their will is broken.* It felt an appropriate conclusion to draw, but he had much more to learn as a Beastling. It seemed as if he had just completed the first step in an otherwise taxing journey.

"How bad is it?" He asked as Horrah knelt beside the boy in the beast's open palm.

"Penetrated through the right shoulder. It is not as dire as Rhen's injury and with less bleeding." She placed her bare palm under his clothing and on his breast. "I'm halting the blood. I think he merely fainted. The organs are giving off their usual pulses. Fear is a powerful weapon and intoxicant. Kael, bring me my supplies. Runith, I need you to lead the beast out of the caverns and out of the boy's calling proximity, should he wake."

"I can, but..." he scratched his head. "I know he is just a lad, but is letting him live worth the risk?"

"How do you plan on learning why a group of Chussmen were scourging our Court's mind with this beast?"

"What do you mean? Do you plan on torturing him?"

He thought he saw a grin begin to rise, despite her somber focus. "No torturing, but we will take him back to Kzhek. A *Feelman* can learn anything we need from him, regardless of his will to comply."

CHAPTER EIGHT

ACQUAINTANCE

Though it took effort, Runith was able to initiate a meaningful conversation with the mole imp. It seemed like an hour had passed since they left the cavern tunnels; traveling through them was much easier when you rely on the speed of a behemoth mole to tunnel straight through.

"Forgive me, but I do not know why the boy forced me to obey."

He turned up to look at the placated creature. All beasts, no matter how ferocious or vile, held their own beauty if seen through a tranquil lens. How odd it was to sit beside a creature that tried to annihilate him on the same day. It felt like sitting in a tavern across from a friend after resolving a dispute.

"No need to worry. I'm sure we'll find a way. Now tell me, mole imp, do you have a name?"

"All beings have names, but I am no mole imp." The beast snorted. Runith felt that he understood it as a laugh. Not only could he understand the languages of beasts, but he had begun to learn their individual mannerisms. *"I am Maest. I do not understand human-speak, but we refer to ourselves as Sklein."* He felt that he could translate Maest's grunted name into common syllables. Communicating with beasts was a new sense that he was working to understand. The mystery of it thrilled him, rather than discouraged.

What else do you ask a creature while waiting for your friends?

"So, do you have any women in your life?"

"I am a female and do not have a single *mate, if that is what you were inquiring about. Humans tend to keep a single relationship, but we are more open with our mating. I have many mates to please me. I am well known for my prowess in—"*

"You know, I think that is enough." He was interested in the Sklein but would rather learn about *other* aspects of their culture. He was no perfect Zhaesman but knew

where boundaries should be drawn to keep him from profanity.

"Do you have any mates?" she asked.

"I don't like that question."

"Forgive my offense."

"No offense taken." He attempted to snort-laugh as she had.

"Are you ill?"

Perd me, best avoid humor for now. *"No, just an itch. Tell me, what is it like being spoken to by one of us in your tongue?"*

"What is it like for you to speak to us?"

"I mean... the Chussboy controlled you, then I did. It looked like you were in pain when we fought over you. What was that like?"

"It is difficult to explain. I would not refer to your speech as 'controlling,' but convincing. It is like following hunger. Sometimes your appetite is a mere bother, while it may otherwise make you a feral being that will obey anything to resolve the hunger. It is more than just voices in our tongue. You humans are able to touch parts of our mind that make us more willing to obey. I do not feel so forced now, but the boy made me act against my inner instincts. He held me for a long while; this was no single event. He is more convincing than you were. It is fortunate that you were able to break his connection."

"More convincing than me?" Runith turned to Maest in shock.

"And more powerful."

"But... he is just a boy! How?"

"It felt like you spoke to me on borrowed energy while he was the source."

Was it true? Could the Endowers hold more power than the Endowed as the Chussmen and Tchoyasmen proclaimed? It was too early to draw conclusions. In the coming years, truth would reveal itself as the Endowers in anti-harvesting Courts grew into adulthood.

Panting echoed from the chamber. Kael shouted and rejoiced over the sunlight, though clouds obscured most of the sky with gray.

Runith stood and proceeded to the mouth of the cave to meet them. Relief filled his veins. The Chussboy, though slightly pale in fear, walked beside them with a cloth binding his mouth.

"Good catch on the binding." said Runith. "We don't need more fighting over Maest."

"Maest?" asked Yeila with the corner of her lip turned up in disgust. "Is that what you've taken to calling it?"

"It's not my name for her. She told me herself."

"Right." she nodded with a roll of her eyes. He was not going to argue with her stone-minded opinions. Yeila was more of a mindless brute than Maest, especially with Yeila's unsightly wounds.

"Back to Kzhek, then?" he asked.

Horrah grasped the boy's shoulder. "Best hand this boy over to a Feelman for interrogation. I am sure Royss has room for *Maest* in the courtyards for whatever he wishes for her. Though I wonder, how are we going to fit her in a carriage?"

"You all can take one back. She's faster than ghete, anyway. I'm sure I can convince her to let me ride on her back."

CHAPTER NINE

DOMESTICATION DILEMMA

A fter the fifth Zhaesman screamed and hid from Maest, Runith decided to circumvent the city to find a less conspicuous way to the Canton of Agriculture. Still, some civilians saw them on their new route, providing a unique story to tell their children. Wild beasts were not unseen near the Canton of Agriculture, but one as big as Maest was a startling exception.

"What a fiend!" Royss shouted with open arms as he walked out to the Canton's courtyard. "You look quite confident up there!"

Runith chuckled and commanded Maest to lower him to the ground. "She's quite the creature. I think we will get some good use out of her."

"We'll have the Scholars come and take a look at it, then I want that head mounted in my hall!"

"You can't be serious, Royss."

"We can't have a thing like that roaming the city."

"I'm sure we can find *some* use for it."

Royss held a scowl until it dissipated into a grin. "We can discuss that later. We at least need some Scholars to see why she might have caused such havoc in the Gleff."

Runith sighed, though recognized that Maest's situation was not yet resolved. "Why invite the Scholars when we have a Chussman to tell us what they were doing there?"

"A *Chuss*man?"

"More of a Chuss*boy*."

"How peculiar. Well, where is he?"

"With the company in the carriage, have they arrived yet?"

"Not that I've seen."

"Well, they should not be far behind."

Royss nodded. "Let's take your beast to the menagerie for now. I suppose we do not need the Scholars to investigate the matter, but I am sure they would insist on taking a look."

Scholars from the Patriarchy, not much more desirable than the Bronze Seers, yet more reliable. "I'll meet you in the council room. I can lead her to the menagerie."

"You know where it is?"

"I'm still the perding captain of the guards over your Canton, Royss. I haven't grown that incompetent."

Royss let out a guttural chuckle. "With your success today, maybe we can see that you are given a higher position. No Endowed should spend his day standing around a Canton. Then again, is that not what we nobles do every day?" He chased his humor with another chortle. "Very well, I will see you in the council room."

"What does he want?" Royss stumbled as he turned back to see Maest grunting to Runith.

"I am to take you to the Canton's menagerie." Runith replied in her tongue.

"I do not understand."

"We are going to place you in a secure area while we decide what to do with you here."

"Why not free me?"

He stared at her with sorrow. Her will persevered. She remained servile yet held onto her oppressed inner desires. *Would it be treasonous to free her? Would she return to her own life, or continue in destruction? Who am I to dictate the future of a being that has her own personal liberties?* His mind was a carriage that found itself against an immovable wall. He would have never assumed to deal with such ethical dilemmas after receiving his graft, and these thoughts did not touch the greater price. *Whose child perished for my gain?*

"*They will keep you there for only a short time. I will see that you have freedom.*"

"*You swear an oath.*"

"*I swear.*" Runith loathed liars and deceivers, yet he worried that he had just become one. His mind returned to the buyak, the first beast that spoke to him about its captivity.

Maest grunted. He was not *afraid* to keep eye contact with her, yet shame provided a greater blockade.

"How was the return on the behemoth's back?" asked Kael as he sat at the grand table in the council room of the Canton of Agriculture. The boy was not one to shirk from his responsibilities, but he still failed to shake off his distressed trembles while on the hunt.

"Best ride of my life," chuckled Runith. After distancing himself from Maest, his enthusiasm had returned. He had not yet buried his problem, only placed it under a veil. "Beats the fastest ghete I've ridden. You should try it, Kael."

"Well... I." There it was, that characteristic timidity. It was no character flaw, only a mere trait that made the boy more approachable. "That thing," Kael turned to Royss, "do we know what it is?"

Royss began to speak from across the table, "well, I figure that we need to ask some Schol–"

"She told me that she is a Sklein." He did not speak the name in Maest's tongue, yet it felt a natural translation, as if he spoke a greeting from an eastern dialect.

"I'm sure we have some name of our *own* for them," replied Royss, "but that, frankly, is not important right now. Runith told me about some Chussboy, said he caused all of this. Where is he?"

"Bound in the Canton of Diplomacy." said Yeila.

"That is hardly the place for a foreign prisoner. It should be to unite the Courts, not divide them further." Royss wiped his face, pulling on his beard with a deep sigh. "*Perd*, if any Chussmen see him there, we will only perpetuate the harvesting conflict."

Yeila failed to react to Royss' worries, remaining like a statue. It seemed an appropriate comparison for her personality as well. "Thane Leisa is going to read the child to see if we might be able to learn why he was controlling the beast."

"Wait, *controlling*? You failed to inform me that he was an Endower, Runith!" Royss swiped in the air as if his questions were pestering insects. "My questions can wait. I need you all to explain this to me and Sheath, or I should say Thane Leisa, when we gather there. When is she expecting us?"

"She seemed more inclined for an immediate visit." Yeila replied.

"Well?" Royss looked around, trying to gather his thoughts. "Best not keep her captive over our captive." He turned to a guard near the doorway. "Zhaesman, have a carriage drawn."

"Yes, Sir. Right away, Sir." He left forthright.

Runith understood the need for haste, but the Canton of Diplomacy was not distant. The ghete carriage was yet another flaunt of luxury to be used by the whim of nobility.

CHAPTER TEN

CARE IS THE CREED

"Is he ready?" Runith asked.

Thane Leisa nodded as she escorted the party to the lower level of the Canton of Diplomacy. "I kept him well fed. Even if he may be a threat, he is still a child."

"An Endower," interjected Royss. "Even if he is young, it is best to treat him as an adult. We still do not know what their abilities entail."

"Runith said he was a Beastling. Is that not clear enough?" Thane Leisa spoke in a lighter tone.

"Are we sure that their physiology follows these rules of our nomenclature? Perhaps he tends to behave as the others we deem 'Beastlings,' yet we lack evidence to prove our theories to be law."

Thane Leisa maintained a forward glare, suppressing a frustrated sigh.

"I agree, Thane Leisa. If he has malicious intentions, they are surely forced upon him by his elders." Runith said, turning to Royss. "He is just a boy, *Sir*."

Royss huffed a laugh, shaking his head with a grin.

Runith agreed but knew that a snark mark could never fail to dispel the tension between the Thanes.

"Are you sure he needs to be read by a Feelman?" she asked, pausing before the chamber door.

"He failed to answer any of my questions," Yeila said.

"It does no harm, right?" said Royss.

"Not that I know of, but people tend to feel uneasy when I—"

"Read their minds?" Runith pitched.

"I cannot read their minds." Thane Leisa replied. "Not exactly."

Royss chuckled, "I've told him to acquaint himself with Endowed. Looks like he still has more to learn about them."

Thane Leisa nodded. "I can only analyze his reactions, facial expressions, verbal intonations, and so forth. I may not be able to read his thoughts, but my Feelman abilities are a close sibling to doing so. Regardless, it can feel invasive to feel as if your innermost secrets are exposed. An individual can become a traitor without uttering a word."

"It does not matter," grunted Royss. "Molest his mind, if you will, he is a threat to Court Zhaes. If anything, we spare him from the blades of more vile forms of inquisition."

Thane Leisa stood in a brief stupor, surrendering to the suggestions of the party and leading them into a dim chamber.

The Canton of Diplomacy was regal in its decor, but it appeared that the architects neglected the lower chambers. Unpainted walls and cracked stone floors whispered that this was not a dungeon only by name. A wide table tread across the room, one scratched and thin that was reminiscent of a cutting board. The stone resonated with a chill that nevertheless led the desert-accommodated Chussboy to sweat and tremble at the entering interrogators.

His dark skin paled to the shade of a Gruthman. His fingers twisted the manacle's chains, his eyes watching them turn penitently.

"I'm sorry," Runith wished to say in some beast tongue that could only be understood between them, yet he remained silent. *Why feel remorse for someone who has used his power for malice? Were his intentions malev-*

olent? He knew not how to accuse the boy, but held some kinship as a Beastling, despite their difference in age and nationality. *Does he look upon me as an annihilator of his kind for taking a grafted organ?* He remained silent, staring at the boy.

Thane Leisa sat in a chair across from the boy while the rest of the company remained standing. Her laxity seemed a nice gesture, but if her skills proved the rumors true, they would be finished with the boy in a few moments.

"I need to provoke his mind," she said. "I cannot read him if he is not thinking about what you want to know."

"Why were you attacking our mines?" asked Yeila.

"No," Thane Leisa shook her head. "No. We need to work up to that. Who is to say that he is *attacking* the Court?"

Yeila sneered. Thane Leisa did not even attempt to read him after her blunt question.

"Let me try." Horrah turned to face the boy. "Why were you in the Cloven Gleff? How many were with you? Who sent you?"

Thane Leisa raised a hand to slow Horrah. She glared into the boy's eyes, though he avoided looking into hers.

The corners of Thane Leisa's mouth turned into a downward arch.

Runith glared at her and at the boy, nearly falling in anticipation. "What is it? Did–"

She raised a hand to silence him, forcing her glare into the youngling's ghastly blue eyes. Not only could Runith feel the startling rise in the Thane, but the boy began to kick, attempting to leave despite his chains.

Thane Leisa exhaled, ready to unload the weight she had taken upon herself.

"Shouldn't we leave him to speak in a more private setting?" Royss asked.

"What would that accomplish? All that I say comes from what I read in him." Royss stared at her blankly. The rest of the company took an additional step inward. She repeated her sigh. "I... I don't know what we will do with him. The Chussmen seem to wish for perpetual conflict over grafting. It seems that he is a part of some radical sect, yet I know that many Chussmen would stand behind their efforts."

"What were they doing in the Gleff?" Runith asked. He glanced at the boy, his cheek shimmering from shameful tears.

"I suppose they saw the foolishness in continuing to riot against our already flourishing system of harvesting. Keep in mind that this is a child with limited political understanding. Using one of their Endowers, they sought to disrupt our infrastructure and economy by disrupting production and mining at the Cloven Gleff."

"This is absurd." Steam billowed in Yeila's frustration. "This is a declaration of war!"

Runith chuckled, and Royss followed, though he muffled it with a feigned cough.

"Settle, Gorger." Sheath said. "These were not noblemen. Unfortunately, the boy had no idea who their company's employer was, but that does not discount the threat. I would not declare war from this occurrence. Extremists are a common occurrence in an ununified land."

"How many were in their party?" Royss asked.

"Difficult to say," remarked Rhen. "We found a single Chussman's corpse in the tunnels leading to the chamber where we found the large beast. I suppose others could have been in other passages or eaten whole by the cavern imps."

"I doubt they would eat the bones." Thane Leisa turned back to the boy. "I cannot place a number on it. I suppose he did not know how large their group was. It seems like anywhere from ten to thirty."

"Does he know what happened to the others?" Runith asked. He tried to offer the boy a pitying grin when he looked up to wipe his tears. A dead stare, absent of emotion, even sorrow, stared back at Runith. He returned the anxious gaze, forgetting to breathe until Thane Leisa continued.

"He was the only one of his kind in the company. I suppose many fell victim to collapsed rock. Others probably fell to the imps."

"I haven't heard any reports of Chussmen in the caverns from my officers at the Gleff." Royss said. "Imps seem the most likely culprit."

Thane Leisa scoffed. "What a waste of a fight. By falling into our possession, they only proved how useful Endowed can be. If this boy makes it back to his home Court, I pray that he will carry a spirit of warning."

Royss furrowed his brow. "You cannot suggest that we send this Beastling back to continue their efforts against us?"

"Are you deaf, Royss? This was a small group, not the Court officials."

"And this is based on your *mystical readings* of a four, five-year-old Chussboy."

"Be careful who you challenge. I can learn anything about you that you have ever thought or done with a glare."

Royss stood back and straightened his shoulders.

"Don't worry. I know how to focus and ignore. I try not to pry into the filth that people tend to hide behind their ego."

They shared a smile, yet Runith still noticed a quiver in Royss' face.

"It is best that you do. I lived a loud life before taking up the title of Thane of Agriculture."

"Loud?" Thane Leisa scoffed. "A loud life by Zhaes standards is saintlier than a Priess philanthropist. What did you do, forget to read the Tome of Measure daily?"

"Something along those lines. Don't you worry, fellow Thane, I've shaped up since then." She opened her eyes wide and began to open her lips until Royss feigned another cough. "Enough of us. In all sincerity, what are we going to do with him?"

"Nothing." she said without a suggestion of hesitancy.

Royss laughed with unnecessary force.

Runith almost caught on, but was held back by Thane Leisa's stare, one more sober than a Zhaes priest. "Surely you jest."

"Not in the slightest," she responded. "We barely passed through the induction of harvesting unscathed. Sending accusations in this fragile period of peace would surely ignite violence."

"Sheath," Royss accused, dropping her title. "We are the victims. We cannot shirk this off as perding pacifists."

"I would rather risk another attack from some radical group than risk the state of our entire Court, if not all of Facet."

"Are you willing to risk so much on the assumption that these were 'some radical group'? What if they *were* sent by the nobility?"

"I need not remind you who read the boy, unless you have become a Feelman yourself, Royss."

Royss' tongue stumbled without a clear rebuttal. No one dared argue. Runith held her eyes, knowing that she read his fears.

Runith stared at the floor. "I would have to agree. I'm no saint, but I'm sure *The Tome of Measure* has some scripture that teaches a saint to take a small beating for the stability of the land. Better for us to suffer a scratch than for the Courts to fall into war. Am I wrong?"

"I cannot recall the verse, but I too recall it." Kael offered him a nod.

"Sheath! You perding kulfs!" Royss turned an accusatory glare to the entire party. "What would have happened if these Chussmen succeeded? We have much more to lose by allowing this to perpetuate."

"An act of grace will quell the flames of contention for now." Thane Leisa remained adamant. Her attitude was even more persuasive than her words. "We have won the right to harvest in four of the six Courts. Do not let your emotions unwind our victory, Royss. War may come in the future as society ages with harvesting, but that is not our matter to deal with now. Laeih in his holiness would have us be the moral superiors."

Royss slumped with his back against the wall, stretching his forehead between his fingers. He remained silent, surrendering with his gestures. Runith had seen his friend frustrated before, but he felt that something had tensed deeper within the Thane of Agriculture. He seemed ready to comply but would spare no mercy should the Chussmen strike again.

Thane Leisa stared down at the crown of his head, reading his submission. "For the sake of peace, this matter concludes here. I will see that the boy is dealt with, but the rest of you are to disperse. Do not speak of this beyond these chambers. This event shall never be recorded unless Royss' presumptions prove true...in the coming years. As of today, no Chussmen ever infiltrated the Cloven Gleff."

EPILOGUE

A pyre burned with a plume of black smoke. The musk of rubble and roasting flesh filled the air. Runith told himself that his tears fell from the heat, yet his fingers ached with a chill.

"You recognized that we could not let that thing roam free." Royss said as flames danced across his eyes in the night.

Runith returned his empty gaze to the fire.

"You seem distraught, Runith. You weren't like this when you brought me back imp heads from your past hunts. Where's the glory in gore?"

Runith snorted, suggesting a smile, but returned to his dry stare. He hadn't spoken with those imps of the past, nor the zeins, nor any of the other supposed menaces he was paid to exterminate. He *had* spoken with Maest. It was the dawn of a friendship, one that was never given the opportunity to bloom. Flame withered her corpse away like salt scattered in a pond.

"Head home. I'll watch over the fire. It's on my property, after all."

Runith shook his head and sat on the rough ground.

"Speak up, you kulf."

He heard Royss but cared not to process his words. His mind was too occupied to pay heed to the entitled Thane.

Family members and friends had passed on. This was not the same sting. He felt it would be similar to losing a comrade in war, but he had never been in war. No living man or woman had. Were the Chussmen's actions suggestive of returning to the barbaric practices of ancient kingdoms? The injustice remained, reducing Maest to ash.

"Runith, you could use some mead. Come in and I'll–"

"I want the buyak. I'll buy it off of you if I need to."

"What?" That tentacled bastard that you spoke to? Did you already drink without me?"

"Get the Seer or whoever owns it. I want it."

"What use could you have for it? You want another thing to slay?"

He slapped away Royss' leather boots as he tried to approach. "Just get it to me. You're the perding Thane. Work it out."

He stood and left Royss to finish tending the fire. He had a promise to fulfill.

༺❀❀❀ ❀❀❀❀༻

Four years later - the present day
Year 332 in the Clerical Era

༺❀❀❀ ❀❀❀❀༻

"You will fare well, Zhaesman." Runith placed a hand on Kael's shoulder. He need not call the boy "boy" any longer. He was a man and had earned the respect of any who graced his presence.

Kael chuckled with his characteristic hesitancy. "If you say so." He straightened the bronze lapel pin on his right breast.

"Being better than me will be an impossible feat, but that does not diminish the challenge." Runith patted Kael's shoulder as he removed his hand and stood. "I have no fear that you will command well. It is serving under Royss that worries me."

"I thought you were close?"

"Of course we are. I know him more than my own kin, that is why I worry about you. He is one of my closest acquaintances yet is a flawed man that dances on the line of Priesslike pride. He could use an honorable captain by his side to sway him towards the righteousness of a proper Zhaesman."

"You are an honorable man, Runith. Surely you were a positive influence."

Runith shrugged and turned his gaze to the passing bystanders. "I try, but I am far from the ideal Zhaesman."

"We all strive for such perfection, do we not?"

Silence filled the following moments. It was not an uncomfortable silence, but one well warranted for sober contemplation. Runith would have sat for an hour or more, but Kael was eager to move on.

"What will you do now? Continue hunting?"

"Something like that. I will no longer labor directly under Royss' jurisdiction, but he is working with the Krall to form some *coalition* of Beastlings. Reason has led me to suspect that Royss fears the return of conflict. I assume you have heard rumors of the riots in Court Sleff."

Kael replied with a perplexed glare.

"Maybe it is just tavern speak. A man like you would do well to stay away from those crowds."

"I can hold my drinks well enough!"

Runith chuckled with a sarcastic nod. His smile dissolved into an unsure bite on his lower lip. "Some claim that mobs have gathered in their capitol to protest harvesting."

"Drunken words for desperate ears, I'm sure."

Runith shrugged.

"Why would they turn away from their only source of value? Without Endowed, they would become as powerless as the vermin that fill their streets!"

"I never said I had the answer, Kael. It is just gossip, gossip with a little more ground than most rumors."

Kael held his shoulders back. Facial hair had started to fill his jaw, now defined by muscle rather than fat.

"You will do well without me pestering you each day. Royss needs a better guard."

Kael chuckled, not even hinting at embarrassment. It made Runith smile. Kael deserved to have a sense of pride by now.

"I'll be part of the Canton. You, Runith, you will be the hero. Remember me when you save Court Zhaes from those ungrateful urchins. Maybe someday you can convince Royss to put me in line for a graft."

"Don't worry. I will remember this day for eras to come." Runith cast his gaze. He was happy for Kael, but his smile fell as he grew sober for his duty. It had been ages since conflict caused war, but he felt that something of the like was awakening in bands that bound the Courts. It was the dawn of a new era, one that would be inscribed in the histories.

The story continues in *Elegy of a Fragmented Vineyard (Paladins of the Harvest #1)*

Afterword

Thank you for taking your time to read this book! As an independent author, your opinion of this book can make a big difference. Please take a few moments to review this book on Goodreads, Amazon, and anywhere else you would like to. If you enjoyed reading this, please tell your friends and family about it and check out my novel, *Elegy of a Fragmented Vineyard*.

ABOUT THE AUTHOR

 Kaden Love wrote his debut novel in his final year of nursing school. Dedicated to his craft, he is ready to begin an epoch of unique fantasy. Inspired by the works of George R. R. Martin, Brandon Sanderson, and Pierce Brown, he wanted to create his own worlds. He currently lives with his wife in Salt Lake City, Utah where he juggles running to audiobooks, writing, reading, and living out his own adventures.

@kadenloveauthor on Instagram, X (Twitter), and TikTok

Website: Kadenrlove.com